This book belongs to

Hello!

Goodbye!

PaRragon

Bath · New York · Cologne · Melbourne · Delhi
Hong Kong · Shenzhen · Singapore · Amsterdam

This edition published by Parragon Books Ltd in 2015 and distributed by

Parragon Inc.
440 Park Avenue South, 13th Floor
New York, NY 10016
www.parragon.com
Please retain this information for future reference.

ISBN 978-1-4748-0390-8

Printed in China

My First 100 WORDS

Illustrated by Paula Knight

My family

Mom

Dad

brother

sister

baby

Grandma

Grandpa

dog

In my home

door

window

rug

television

chair

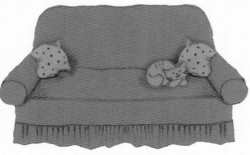
sofa

table

flowers

Getting dressed

undershirt

underpants

shorts

pants

 skirt    socks    shoes    shirt    sweater

Mealtime

bowl

plate

pitcher

knife

 fork

 spoon

 cup

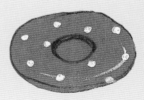 saucer

Playtime

train   trumpet    drum    blocks

 jack-in-the-box  doll  paints  puzzle

In the city

bus

truck

store

bicycle

car

stroller

fire truck

motorcycle

In the park

swings   slide   seesaw   ball

ate   tree   bird   kite

At the beach

 pail

 shovel

 ice cream

 fish

 sandcastl

 T-shirt  crab  boat shell

At the market

 basket

 cart

 bananas

 apples

 oranges

 carrots    bread   tomatoes    milk    cheese

On the farm

horse   cow   farmer   pig

hen

cat

sheep

tractor

Bathtime

toothbrush

toothpaste

bathtub

duck   soap   towel   potty   sink

Bedtime

lamp

slippers

bed

clock

book

moon

pajamas

teddy bear

Months of the year

January
February
March
April
May
June
July
August
September
October
November
December

Days of the week

Monday
Tuesday
Wednesday
Thursday
Friday

Saturday
Sunday

Numbers

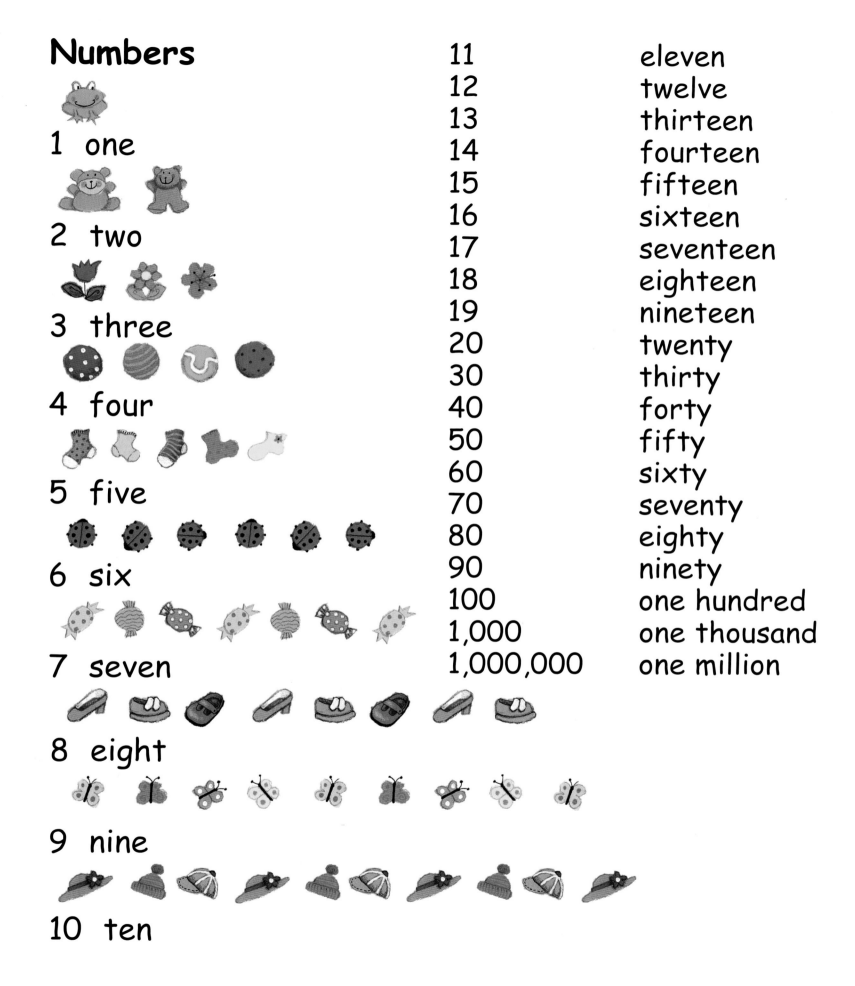

1 one

2 two

3 three

4 four

5 five

6 six

7 seven

8 eight

9 nine

10 ten

11 eleven
12 twelve
13 thirteen
14 fourteen
15 fifteen
16 sixteen
17 seventeen
18 eighteen
19 nineteen
20 twenty
30 thirty
40 forty
50 fifty
60 sixty
70 seventy
80 eighty
90 ninety
100 one hundred
1,000 one thousand
1,000,000 one million

Parts of the body

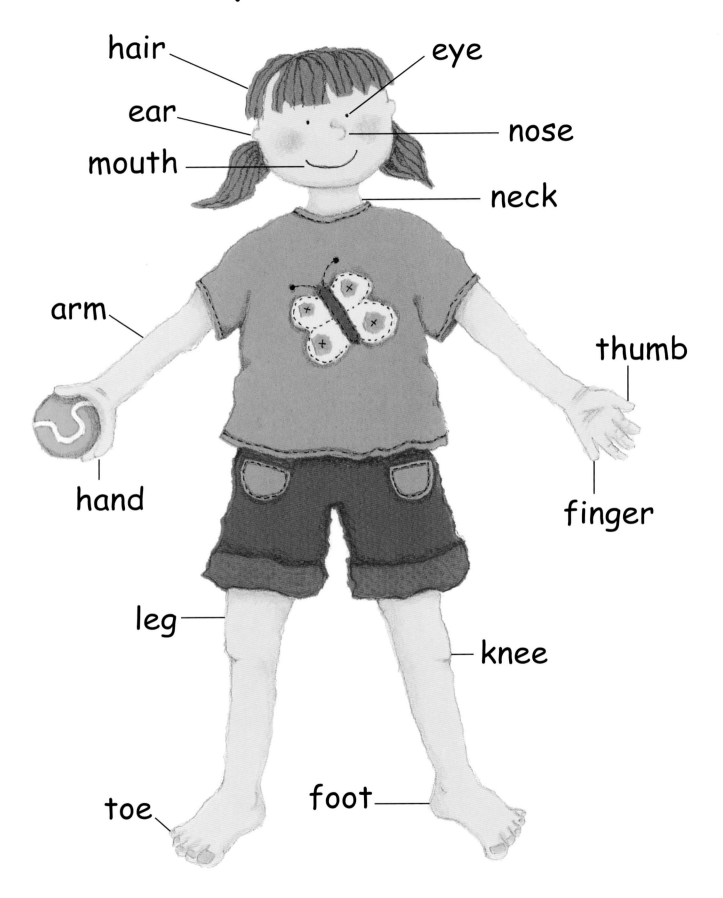

hair

eye

ear

nose

mouth

neck

arm

thumb

hand

finger

leg

knee

toe

foot

Colors

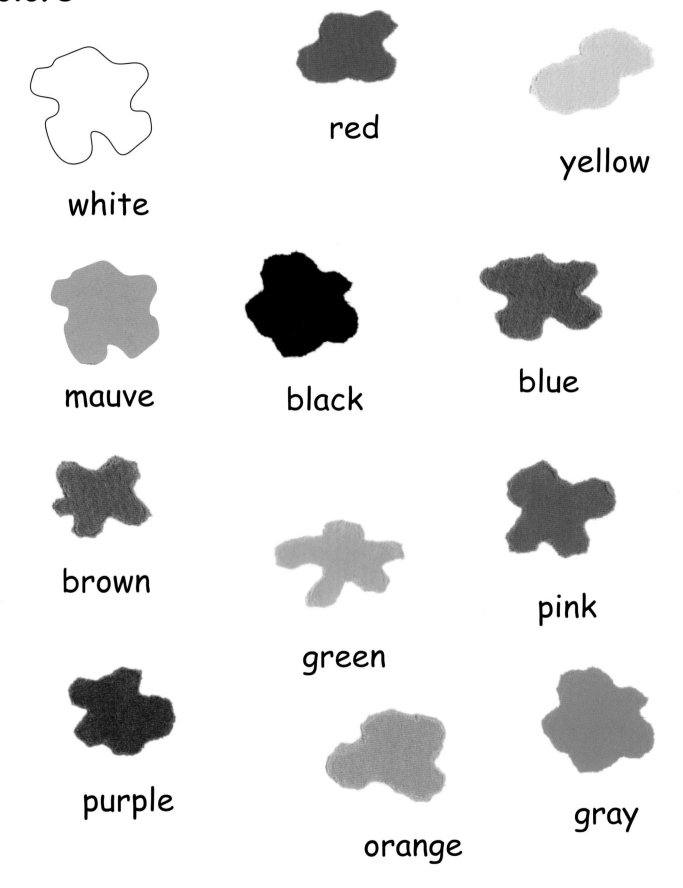

white

red

yellow

mauve

black

blue

brown

green

pink

purple

orange

gray

Matching pairs

Can you match each picture pair?

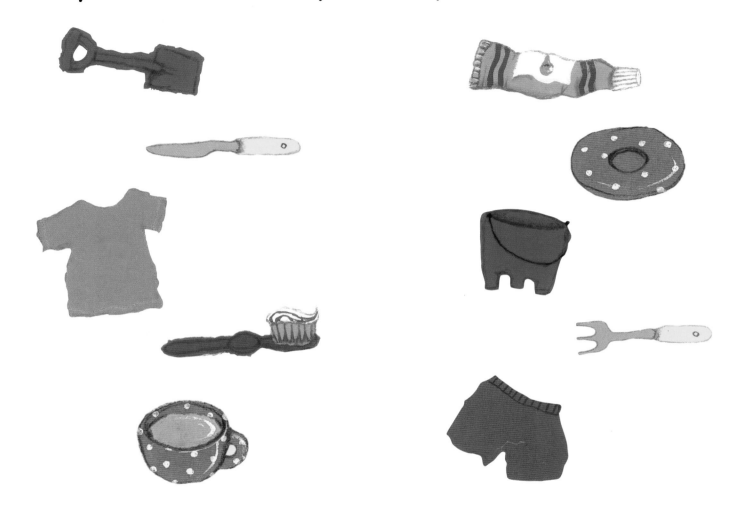

Find the correct picture to match each word below.